This book belongs to:

Contents

Cover illustration and illustrations on
pages 32-33 by Peter Stevenson

Published by Ladybird Books Ltd
80 Strand London WC2R 0RL
A Penguin Company

8 10 9

© LADYBIRD BOOKS LTD MCMXCVII, MMI

LADYBIRD and the device of a Ladybird are trademarks of Ladybird Books Ltd

*All rights reserved. No part of this publication may be reproduced, stored in
a retrieval system, or transmitted in any form or by any means, electronic,
mechanical, photocopying, recording or otherwise, without the prior consent
of the copyright owner.*

ISBN-13: 978-0-72142-381-4
Printed in China

Mystery tour

written by Shirley Jackson
illustrated by Peter Stevenson

Let's go up the road,

up the hill and

down the hill and

round the trees and

over the river and

under the bridge...

to the funfair!

Put that back!

written by Lorraine Horsley

illustrated by Andrew Warrington

11

Can I have some
sweets?

Can I have
a comic?

15

Can I have an
ice cream?

Hey!
That's cheating!

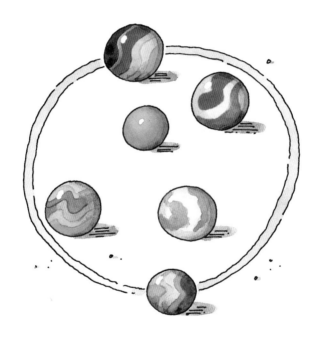

written by Marie Birkinshaw

illustrated by Graham Round

One for me and

one for you.

Two for me and

one for you.

Three for me and

one for you.

Wheels

written by Marie Birkinshaw
illustrated by David Parkins

One wheel,

two wheels,

three wheels,

four.

Four wheels?

Two wheels!

Four wheels no more!

New words introduced in this book

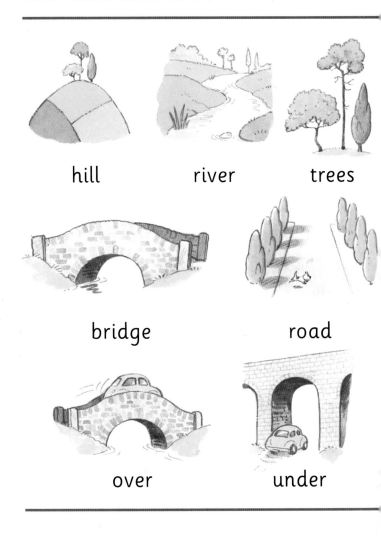

hill river trees

bridge road

over under

can, cheating, have, hey

Hey! That's cheating!

This story introduces the numbers one to four, which are reinforced in the next rhyme, *Wheels*.
Ask your child to read the speech bubbles in voices that he thinks the boys would use.

Wheels

Try saying this to the rhythm of *One potato, two potato*... You may like to try making up other counting rhymes like this.

New words

These are the words that help to tell the stories and rhymes in this book. Try looking through the book together to find some of the words again. (Vocabulary used in the titles of the stories and rhymes is not listed.)

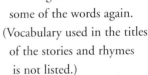

Read with Ladybird

Read with Ladybird has been written to help you to help your child:

- to take the first steps in reading
- to improve early reading progress
- to gain confidence

Main Features

- **Several stories and rhymes in each book**

This means that there is not too much for you and your child to read in one go.

- **Rhyme and rhythm**

Read with Ladybird uses rhymes or stories with a rhythm to help your child to predict and memorise new words.

- **Gradual introduction and repetition of key words**

Read with Ladybird introduces and repeats the 100 most frequently used words in the English language.

- **Compatible with school reading schemes**

The key words that your child will learn are compatible with the word lists that are used in schools. This means that you can be confident that practising at home will support work done at school.

- **Information pullout**

Use this pullout to understand more about how you can use each story to help your child to learn to read.

But the most important feature of **Read with Ladybird** is for you and your child to have fun sharing the stories and rhymes with each other.

   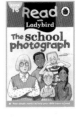

Learning to read with this book

Mystery tour

As this story introduces important words that your
child has not met before (over, under), it is a good idea
to read this story to your child first.

Put that back!

A lot of the words in this story are the same; only one
or two of the words change on every other page.
Read this story to your child and encourage him to
join in with the speech bubbles.
Can your child see where the
streamer gets caught
on Mum's trolley?